The Poetry Of Edgar Wallace

WRIT IN BARRACKS - A volume of poems, mostly about the British Army during the Boer War.

Richard Horatio Edgar Wallace was born on the 1st April 1875 in Greenwich, London. Leaving school at 12 because of truancy, by the age of fifteen he had experience; selling newspapers, as a worker in a rubber factory, as a shoe shop assistant, as a milk delivery boy and as a ship's cook.

By 1894 he was engaged but broke it off to join the Infantry being posted to South Africa. He also changed his name to Edgar Wallace which he took from Lew Wallace, the author of *Ben-Hur*.

In Cape Town in 1898 he met Rudyard Kipling and was inspired to begin writing. His first collection of ballads, *The Mission that Failed!* was enough of a success that in 1899 he paid his way out of the armed forces in order to turn to writing full time.

By 1904 he had completed his first thriller, *The Four Just Men*. Since nobody would publish it he resorted to setting up his own publishing company which he called Tallis Press.

In 1911 his Congolese stories were published in a collection called *Sanders of the River*, which became a bestseller. He also started his own racing papers, *Bibury's* and *R. E. Walton's Weekly*, eventually buying his own racehorses and losing thousands gambling. A life of exceptionally high income was also mirrored with exceptionally large spending and debts.

Wallace now began to take his career as a fiction writer more seriously, signing with Hodder and Stoughton in 1921. He was marketed as the 'King of Thrillers' and they gave him the trademark image of a trilby, a cigarette holder and a yellow Rolls Royce. He was truly prolific, capable not only of producing a 70,000 word novel in three days but of doing three novels in a row in such a manner. It was in, estimating that by 1928 one in four books being read was written by Wallace, for alongside his famous thrillers he wrote variously in other genres, including science fiction, non-fiction accounts of WWI which amounted to ten volumes and screen plays. Eventually he would reach the remarkable total of 170 novels, 18 stage plays and 957 short stories.

Wallace became chairman of the Press Club which to this day holds an annual Edgar Wallace Award, rewarding 'excellence in writing'.

Diagnosed with diabetes his health deteriorated and he soon entered a coma and died of his condition and double pneumonia on the 7th of February 1932 in North Maple Drive, Beverly Hills. He was buried near his home in England at Chalklands, Bourne End, in Buckinghamshire.

TO THE RANK AND FILE OF THE ROYAL ARMY MEDICAL CORPS AMONGST WHOM I SPENT SIX HAPPY YEARS OF MY LIFE, THIS COLLECTION OF VERSES MOSTLY WRITTEN IN BARRACKS IS ADMIRINGLY DEDICATED
RONDEBOSCH, April 4, 1900

Index Of Poems

WAR

I

A tent that is pitched at the base:
A wagon that comes from the night:
A stretcher—and on it a Case:
A surgeon, who's holding a light.
The Infantry's bearing the brunt—
O hark to the wind-carried cheer!
A mutter of guns at the front:
A whimper of sobs at the rear.
And it's War! "Orderly, hold the light.
You can lay him down on the table: so.
Easily—gently! Thanks—you may go."
And it 's War! but the part that is not for show.

II

A tent, with a table athwart,
A table that's laid out for one;
A waterproof cover—and nought
But the limp, mangled work of a gun.
A bottle that's stuck by the pole,
A guttering dip in its neck;
The flickering light of a soul
On the wondering eyes of The Wreck,
And it's War. "Orderly, hold his hand.
I 'm not going to hurt you, so don't be afraid.
A ricochet! God! what a mess it has made!"
And it's War! and a very unhealthy trade.

III

The clink of a stopper and glass:
A sigh as the chloroform drips:
A trickle of—what? on the grass,
And bluer and bluer the lips.
The lashes have hidden the stare....
A rent, and the clothes fall away....
A touch, and the wound is laid bare....
A cut, and the face has turned grey....
And it's War! "Orderly, take It out.
It's hard for his child, and it's rough on his wife.
There might have been—sooner—a chance for his life.
But it's War! And—Orderly, clean this knife!"

ARMY DOCTOR

Army Doctor! Army Doctor!
'Ere's some 'cruities for inspection,
Some in rags, an' some in cuffs.
Some in shirts, an' some without 'em,
Wot a blessed strange collection!
Served before? You needn't doubt 'em,
Bloomin' muffs!

Army Doctor! Army Doctor!
Take your sword, an' drop your lancet,
Teach your nurses 'ow to fight!
'Ow to march the dead march—solemn!
'Ow to route march—an' to dance it!
Teach 'em 'ow to march in column.
By the right!

Army Doctor! Army Doctor!
Gold an' velvet! 'broidered lacin's,
'Oldin' 'igh your bloomin' 'ead!
'Seen you peel that coat so winnin',
'Seen you stain them pretty facin's,

'Seen your 'ighly glossy linen.
Splattered red!

Army Doctor! Army Doctor!
'Sun is 'ot—an' we are learnin'
Lessons in the cholera school,
We're fear-sick, an' mad as 'atters.
Throat a-parchin', 'ead a-burnin'.
Seems to me, you're takin' matters
Rather cool!

Army Doctor! Army Doctor!
Spurs and swagger! Cuff an' collar!
Up to ev'ry bloomin' trick!
'Seen you—as I've seen none other—
Go to—where I dursn't foller!
'Seen you act the man and brother
To the sick!

Army Doctor! Army Doctor!
Things by Engineers forgotten.
You 'ave got to recollect.
Tho' you're such a gilded dandy,
When the meat is goin' rotten.
Chances are, you're somewhere 'andy
To inspect!

Army Doctor! Army Doctor!
Where the firin' never ceases.
Where the 'uddled soldier lies.
Where the Mauser bullets shave 'im,
Gawd! they're chippin' 'im to pieces!
Git 'im out of fire an' save 'im....
Well done, Guys!

NICHOLSON'S NEK
They gave their best at Waterloo,
For the honour of England's name;
They threw their best on a hundred fields,
To put our foes to shame.
'Tis good that England's soldier men
To-day can do the same.

They have proved their worth,
To the ends of the earth.
They have striven and won,—and failed!
They have shown their might.
On the Dargai Height,
When the mollah's bullets hailed.

They have laid their dead,
In the river bed.
On the site of their last brave stand.
They have buried at night.
By a lantern light,
In a grave that they scooped in the sand.

And far and wide,
They have done and died.
By donga, and veldt, and kloof.
And the lonely grave,
Of the honoured brave.
Is a proof—if we need a proof,
They won—and died,
And we glorified
The men of the barrack schools.
They died—and failed.
And in wrath we railed
At the fault of the bungling fools!

And perhaps it is good
That we change our mood,
And perchance it is well to blame.
And to seek elsewhere,
For some men to bear,
The weight of our foolish shame.
But the fight hard fought,
Must it go for nought
Because of its hapless turn?
Must we then withhold,
For the life hard sold.
The Honour it died to earn?

When hot and tired.
With the last round fired.
And never a ray of hope—
What then the shame?
They were just the same
Who charged Talana's slope!
You may give and take,
As the shrapnels rake,
When your batt'ry has replied;
But you cannot live
When there's too much give.
From the guns on the open side.

Good men are they.
Who gain the day,—
And victory is sweet,—
And just as brave
Who do not rave

At every small defeat.
For the fight hard fought
Must not go for nought,
Because of its hapless turn;
Nor we withhold.
For the life hard sold.
The Honour it died to earn.

We gave our best at Waterloo,
For the honour of England's name;
We threw our best on a hundred fields
To put our foes to shame.
'Tis good that England's soldier men
To-day can do the same.

MY PAL, THE BOER

We met without appointment on an 'ill,
I comed upon the beggar without warnin';
Layin' down be'ind a boulder,
With 'is rifle to 'is shoulder.

He sent along wot's Dutch for a "Good-mornin.'"
'E missed me with a fair amount of skill,
An' 'fore 'e 'd time to mount, an' get from danger,
I was takin' of my rest
By a sittin' on 'is chest,
An' a sayin' to the welcome little stranger:—

"My pal, the Boer!
You're a prisoner of war."
('E tried to break my jaw, but that's a trifle);
"You can't escape me, can yer?
In the name of Rule Britannia,
I commandeer your 'orse an' Mauser rifle!"

You wouldn't call 'is manners over bright.
An' you wouldn't term 'is disposition sunny.
An' 'e 'ad a silly notion
That the cause of the commotion
Was Chamberlain a-fightin' for 'is money;
An' 'e fancied that the British flag was white—
'Twas a silly fancy—still we must excuse it,
When the Lancers came along
'E felt a trifle bong!
'E soon found out the proper way to use it!

My pal, the Boer,
Ain't used to proper war,
But tho' 'e scorns the flag an' does the grandy,

The 'igh an' mighty scorner.
When we get 'im in a corner^

'E FINDS A FLAG OF TRUCE IS MIGHTY 'ANDY!

SONG OF THE FIRST TRAIN THROUGH

Line Clear to Witteputs! I wind around the guarded hill.
And thunder o'er the lean long bridge that spans the sombre stream;
No uptorn rail to devastate, no culvert gap to fill.
And where the outpost feared to ride, I gather up my steam.

(I passed a little mound of earth that bore the cross's sign--
A Colonel, and a dozen men, who fell to clear the line.)

Line Clear to Belmont: and I feel the ballast shaking down:
My flanges bite the new-laid rail and prove the new-thrust pin.
On either side the purple ridge, the veldt land sickly brown,
The "distant off" says "Welcome," and the "Home" says "Come ye in."

(Two thousand guardsmen rushed the Kop—a score are buried here,
And here are laid some Fusiliers—they fell to give Line Clear.)

Line Clear to Graspan: so I run adown the gentle grade.
Nor notice in my joyful haste the kopje stubble grown,
And wildly bouldered foot to crest where fell a half brigade.
What time the bristling mountain-side with segment shell was sown.

(The mess-deck and the ward-room thinned to give the line pratique
Line Clear from Graspan—so, half-mast the Ensign at the Peak.)

Line Clear: along the new-spliced wires that droop from pole to pole.
By Enslin, where the helio glared fitfully and fleet.
The word is passed across the plain to where the rivers roll,—
To where, tree-fringed in eddying swirls, the Modder meets the Riet.

(In heat and thirst and weariness a hundred dying lay,
A hundred bloody forms grew stiff to give me Right Away.)

Line Clear: I face the grim gaunt range that stretches east and west
('Twas by its base, near Magers farm, that Wauchope's men went down):
I skirt the ridge that hid the guns, and gleefully I breast
The easy rise that brings in view the long-beleaguered town.

(Line Clear: o'er blood, and sweat, and fain, and sorrow's road I ran.
And every sleeper was a wound, and every rail a man.)

THE NAVAL BRIGADE

When you're pickin' your men for a fight,

When choosin' the corps that'll serve.
It's only quite proper an' right
To fix upon muscle an' nerve,
An' so, to your heavy Dragoons
Your Granny-dear Guards an' their band
To your Sappers with bridgin' pontoons.
You can buckle the Lower Deck Hand!

(The Lower Deck Hand
Doesn't want any band;
He's grit, an he's sand
Is the Lower Deck Hand.)

His march is a go-as-you-please;
He most keeps step with hisself!
For his boots ain't conducive to ease,
Bein' mostly kept packed on a shelf!
Tho' he isn't so span or so spic
Tho' his marchin' ain't what you 'd call grand
He gets to the front just as quick
Does the elegant Lower Deck Hand!

(The Lower Deck Hand
Wasn't reared in the Strand;
But he's good to command,
Is the Lower Deck Hand.)

You may swear by the jolly marines,
"Per marey, per tarey" they fight—
Not speakin' for them in their 'teens
I don't mind admittin' your right.
But all that the Joey has got.
As I'd have all the world understand,
He's learnt—well, he's learnt quite a lot
From his tooter—the Lower Deck Hand!

(The Lower Deck Hand
Is a mine that's unpanned;
An he's yours to command,
Is the Lower Deck Hand.)

He doesn't shape well at Reviews,
I've known him to spit in the ranks;
But we've never been asked to excuse
A fault, when he's guarding the flanks.
An' when there's a break in the square
Or a place where the Line cannot stand,
I'll tell you the chap to put there—
"Jack Mullow"—the Lower Deck Hand.

(The Lower Deck Hand

Will die as he'll stand;
He's tempered an tan'd,
Is the Lower Deck Hand.)

When you're hemmed in a tight little hole,
By a greatly outnumbering foe,
It's a matter of stokin' an' coal
How far we're away from the foe.
When the Infantry's needin' some aid.
When the 'tillery gets under-man'd,—
Make way for the Naval Brigade!—
His Highness the Lower Deck Hand!

(The Lower Deck Hand
With his guns he can land,
An he'll kick up some sand,
Will the Lower Deck Hand.)

THE ARMOURED TRAIN

There's risk on the ballasted roadway,
There's death on the girdered bridge.
Red ruin from sleeper to sleeper.
And wreck on the bouldered ridge.
No signal to herald my coming,
No whistle to waken the plain;
Stand clear—I am out for patrolling!
Make way for the Armoured Train!

I run not to time, nor to table,
I'm neither an "Up" nor a "Down,"
But "Full speed ahead" is my order.
When skirting the enemy's town.
My mails have a backing of cordite.
My luggage is powder and shell,
With smoke-stack a-blazing I thunder,
A traveller's sample of Hell!

They have laid me a mine by a culvert.
They have loosened a bolt by a curve.
But thrice-tested steel is my muscle,
And thrice-tested brass is my nerve.
A curse for their bungling folly,
A laugh for the death-trap that fails,
A hang for the enemy's miner.
So long as I keep to the rails.

A cheer—and I pull from the township
To spy out the enemy's line;
A plunge—and I rush into darkness

As reckless of wreckage as mine.
And what if a rail has been lifted?
And what if a river's unspanned?
I fail, but I know in the failing
I strove at the Empire's command.

They were men who at Badajos conquered.
They were men who for Wellington struck,
And a Man is the Man at the Throttle,
And a Man is the Man on the Truck.
Undismayed I may go to destruction.
For I know at the end I may feel
I die with the men on the footplate,
I pass with my brothers in steel.

MAKE YOUR OWN ARRANGEMENTS
First published in the Pall Mall Gazette

When the depôt soldier's dinin' on three-quarters of a pound.
If there's too much bone to please 'im, or the meat is extry tough,
'E 'as got a chance of grousin' when 'is orficer goes round,
'E can draw upon the mess-book, if's rations ain't enough.
But it's make your own arrangements! Make your own arrangements!
When you're cut orf from the column, an' supplies are runnin' low.
It ain't no "too much fat, sir!"
But it's bread—an' glad of that, sir!
O it's bake your own arrangements—out of flour—as you go!

When the depôt soldier's on parade 'e sparkles an' 'e shines.
When the depôt soldier's drillin' 'e must make each motion "tell."
When the depôt soldier's marchin' 'e must march on drill-book lines.
'E 'as got a drill-instructor, an' 'e does it very well.
But it's make your own arrangements! Make your own arrangements!
When the camp is rushed at midnight, an' you're fallin' in—to die!
O there ain't no drill-rules set there.
But it's take your gun—an' get there!
When you make your own arrangements, you must grab your belt an' fly.

The depôt soldier's grounded in a systematic drill;
'E also knows wot's "rendezvous" an' what is "bivouac"—
'E knows the use of rifle-pits, the proper way to kill—
'E understands the principles an' the'ries of attack.
But it's make your own arrangements! Make your own arrangements!
When you're dodgin' tons of boulder, climbin' mount'ins under fire.
An' the drill-book won't assist you
Till the fallin' rocks 'ave missed you!
So you make your own arrangements—an' you climb a little 'igher!

When the depôt soldier's wantin' with 'is orficer to speak,

'E must 'alt two paces from 'im, an' salute before the start.
An' 'e mustn't try to argue, an' 'e mustn't give no cheek;
An' if 'is Captain slangs 'im—'e must take it in good part.
But it's make your own arrangements! Make your own arrangements!
When you see 'im lying wounded, all the circumstances change.
An' you don't 'eed no instructions;
An' you don't need introductions;
But you make your own arrangements—an' you get 'im out of range.

When the depôt soldier sickens, when the depot soldier dies,
'E is buried by 'is comrades in the regulation style.
'E is covered by an ensign of the regulation size.
An' 'e gets a firin' party made of thirteen rank an' file.
But it's make your own arrangements! Make your own arrangements!
When the Colonel reads the service by a guard-room lantern light.
When in silent rows you 've laid 'em
In a trench your bay' nets made 'em,
O, it's make your own arrangements when you bury in the night!

GINGER JAMES
A spell I 'ad to wait
Outside the barrick gate.
For Ginger James was passin' out as I was passin' in;
'E was only a recruit,
But I give 'im the salute,
For I'll never git another chance of givin' it agin!

'E'd little brains, I'll swear,
Beneath 'is ginger 'air,
'Is personal attractions, well, they wasn't very large;
'E was fust in ev'ry mill.
An' a foul-mouthed brute, but still
We'll forgive 'im all 'is drawbacks—'e 'as taken 'is discharge.

'E once got fourteen days,
For drunken, idle ways.
An' the Colonel said the nasty things that colonels sometimes say;
'E called him to 'is face
The regiment's disgrace—
But the Colonel took 'is 'at off when 'e passed 'im by to-day.

For days 'e used to dwell
Inside a guard-room cell.
Where they put the darbies on 'im for a 'owlin' savage brute;
But as by the guard 'e went
They gave 'im the present.
The little bugler sounded off the 'General Salute.'

The band turned out to play

Poor Ginger James away;
'Is Captain an' 'is Company came down to see 'im off;
An' thirteen file an' rank.
With three rounds each of blank;
An' 'e rode down on a carriage, like a bloomin' city toff!

'E doesn't want no pass,
'E's journeying first-class;
'Is trav'ling rug's a Union Jack, which isn't bad at all;
The tune the drummers play
It ain't so very gay.
But a rather slow selection, from a piece that's known as 'Saul.'

"HER MAJESTY HAS BEEN PLEASED—"

Wot a crowd of people!
Wot a sea of faces!
'Ow the ladies' parasols are glist'nin' in the sun!
Troops in "open order,"
Captains in their places.
Wish the day was over, and I wish the job was done!

Wot a lot of civvies!
Mus' be 'arf the city!
Like a mob on Boxing-night outside Drury Lane!
Ain't it perfect weather?
More's the blessed pity!
Wish instead of sunshine it was pourin' 'ard o' rain!

Comes of bein' famous—
Mentioned in despatches!
Comes of me a-carrying the Major to the rear!
Empty stomach fighting—
Getting sleep by snatches!—
'Ow the troops must cuss me for a-keeping them out 'ere!

'Ow the people eye me,
Like a choice chrysanth'um!
'Ow this collar's chokin' me!—Lord! I 'm feelin' sick!
Troops are at fhe "shoulder"—
"Pre-sent"—there's the anthem!
'Ow I 'ope 'er Majesty will get it over quick!

Wonder if I'm dusty?
'Elmet feels lopsided!
Chuck a chest for 'Eaven's sake! Lord, I'm feelin' queer!

Twenty times they 've brushed me,
Twice 'ave I been tidied,
Yet I 'm feelin' mucky still. Private Jawkins? 'ERE!

Face the lan-dow panels.
Dumbly; likewise blindly,
Seein' in a sorter mist a lady dressed in black:

'Ear 'er softly talkin'.
Thanks, mum, thank you kindly!
Saw the Major fallin', and I 'ad to take 'im back!
Thank you, mum—your 'Ighness—
Majesty, I mean, mum!
'M sure I'm much obliged to you for this 'ere pretty Cross!

Bless you, you're a lady!
Mean you are the Queen, mum!
On'y picked the Major up an' shoved 'im on an 'orse!
'Saw our Sub go under,
'Alf 'is men around 'im
Cut to bits—an' 'im so young,—yes mum, very sad.

Yes mum, 'e was buried
In the place we found 'im.
Thank you, mum,—your Majesty (God, I 'm feelin' bad!)

ARTHUR

'Oo's the Gen'ral 'ere? sez I;
'Oo's the Gen'ral 'ere?
"O, 'e's a Prince o the Royal Blood,
so you 'aven't got nothin' to fear."
But 'e marched me 'ere, an' 'e marched me there.
To burn blank cartridges everywhere;
An 'e made me sweat, an' 'e made me swear—
Did Arthur!

Wot can the Gen'ral do? sez I;
Wot can the Gen'ral do?
"O, 'e's a Prince o' the Royal Blood,
an' 'e don't know much about you!"
But 'e doubled me round on a big field day:
An' 'e checked me for loafin'—a mile away!
An' I found there's a time for work an' play
With Arthur!

Wot 'as the Gen'ral done, sez I?
Wot 'as the Gen'ral done?
"O, 'e's a Prince o' the Royal Blood,
an' they chucked 'im 'is rank for fun!"
But that was a lie, for I found out since
'E's ninepence a soldier an' thruppence a prince!
'E stood fire in Egypt, an' 'e didn't wince!
Not Arthur!

Wot does the Gen'ral know? sez I;
Wot does the Gen'ral know?
"O, 'e's a Prince o' the Royal Blood,
an' 'e's on'y got up for show!"
But I "chanced" kit inspection, an' thought it a "cert";
But 'e put me down, smart, for a tunic an' shirt!
An', insult to injury—checked me for dirt!
Did Arthur!

'Ow is 'e liked by you? sez I;
'Ow is 'e liked by you?
"O, 'e's a Prince o' the Royal Blood,
but I reckon some'ow 'e'll do!"
I'm willin' to risk, as I've done before,
A Fox 'Ills fight, or a native war.
Or front rank man in an Army Corps,
With Arthur!

Wot is 'e, after all? sez I;
Wot is 'e, after all?
"O, 'e's a swaddie, the same as you,
an' 'e goes to the "orficers' call"!'
'E's a gentleman, Tommy, when all's said an' done!
'Is ma is the lady 'oo's second to none.
An' we love 'er the better because of 'er son—
That's Arthur!

LEGACIES

The dog is yours; and so's the photo frames.
Them pictures wot I cut, an' my new box.
The pack of cards, the dominoes, an' games.
The knittin' needles, an' the knitted socks.
An' all, except the letters and the ring—
You'll find them all together tied with string.

My public clothin'—that goes back to stores—
My kit'll sell by auction on the square;
An' other fellers will be "formin' fours"
An' "markin' time" in boots I used to wear.
They're welcome; but you won't forget to send
The ring an' all the letters to my friend."

The pain ain't near so bad as wot it were
The day they dragged me from the limber wheels;
Ain't I a wreck! for God's sake don't tell 'er;
Say it was fever—peaaeful—in the 'ills;
An' write about the wreaths, the "Jack," and band.
An'—send a bit of hair: you understand?

The ring—Oh no, the doctor lets me talk,
I ain't a-tirin'—'cept a funny light.
An' just a feelin' that I 'd like to walk
To where it seems to flicker in the night.
Better for me to go with aching 'ead.
Than go in trouble with my say unsaid.

The ring—it ain't long since she sent it back;
I never meant no 'arm, God only knows.
But things—I can't tell now—looked very black.
And she believed the others—I suppose,
I'm sorry for 'er now—that cursed wheel!—
You see she is a woman, an' she'll feel.

The dog is yours, I told you that before.
The spurs you'll find 'em in my private kit.
The letters, an' the ring, an' nothin' more,—
An' hair—it's foolish—but a little bit.

"Our Father"—Lord, how strange! It's all-ri'—sir.

The- lett- an'- th'- ring- an'- hair- for- 'er!

T.A. IN LOVE

Dreamin' of thee! Dreamin' of thee!
Sittin' with my elbow on my knee.
I orter be a polishin' the meat-dish an' the can—
(I orter draw the groceries—for I am ord'ly man!
But wot are bloomin' ration calls, an' wot's a pot or pan.
When I'm dreamin'j O my darlin' one, of thee?)

Dreamin' of thee! Dreamin' of thee!
Firin' at the rifle range I be.
I've missed a fust-class targit—an' I've missed the 'ill be'ind!
I nearly shot a marker once! (which wasn't very kind);
The orficer 'e swears at me—but re'ly, I don't mind!
I am dreamin', O my darlin' one, of thee!

Dreamin' of thee! Dreamin' of thee!
Me, as was the smartest man in "B"!
My kit is all untidy, and it's inches thick in dust;
An' my rifle's fouled an' filthy, an' my bay'nit's red with rust;
They've tried to find the reason—but I've seen 'em furder fust!
An' they never guess I'm dreamin', dear, of thee!

Dreamin' of thee! Dreamin' of thee!
They can't make out wot's comin' over me.
The fellows think I'm barmy, an' the Major thinks it's drink,

The Sergeant thought it laziness, so shoved me in the clink!
The Colonel called it "thoughtlessness," so gave me time to think.
An' to dream again, my darlin' one, of thee!

Dreamin' of thee! Dreamin' of thee!
Wot's two 'ours' sentry-go to me?
A sittin' in the sentry-box, a-thinkin' of your eyes,
The ord'ly orficer come along an' took me by surprise!
'E said as I was sleepin'—an' the usual orfice lies!
When I was on'y dreamin', love, of thee!

Dreamin' of thee! Dreamin' of thee!
Rubbin' tarry oakum on my knee!
Oh, when I weigh that oakum in, I know I'll cop it 'ot!
I'll be 'auled before the Gov'nor, an' I'll git an 'our's shot;
But whether I git punishment, or whether I do not.
They can't prevent me dreamin', love, of thee!

TOMMY ADVISES

Take your rifle from the rack:
Take your bay'nit from the shelf;
Clean your straps for marchin' order^
An' git ready for the Border.
For it ain't no sham attack.
So you needn't kid yourself.
It's a ball an' bay'nit action
With the perfect satisfaction
Of a medal, an' a ribbon, and perhaps a clasp or two.
For a-doin' of the little job your betters couldn't do.

Pack your socks, an' fold your shirt.
Wash your water-bottle out.
It'll make your marchin' easy
If your boots are nice an' greasy,—
An' some dubbin wouldn't 'urt.
You can chuck your weight about;
There's an 'appy day before you,
When the civvies will adore you.
And the things wot used to shock 'em will be favoured with a smile.
And your little faults an' failin's won't be noticed for a while.

Git a guernsey out of store—
Winter's very cold above.
An' the wind an' rain will find you
If you leave your clothes behind you!
Trust your pretty self before
Any Quartermaster's love;
For there's no store to go unto
An' no tailors' shops to run to;

For it ain't no ten days' skirmish these manoeuvres wot you're in.
An' a little flannel weskit 'ides a multitood of skin!

Write your letters for the mail;
Tell your people all the news—
For your folks'll prize the writin'
Of 'my son who's out a-fightin'.'
Don't you spin an awful tale.
Just to give your mother blues,
For the day the boys are cryin'
"List o' wounded, dead and dyin'!"

Will be tons of time for them at 'ome to feel a trifle blue.
When they see a dozen Smiths are killed—and wonder which is you!

THE NUMBER ONE

The number one, 'e's on the bridge.
There's goin' to be a row.
The Gold Coast is upon our port.
An', 'ull down, on our bow,
Makin' for 'ome for all she's worth
A slaver's bloomin' dhow!

The number one is on the bridge.
The buntin' tosser's aft;
An' down below, in the 'eat an' glow.
The men are at their graft.
They've peeled their shirts, to get the steam,
To over-'aul that craft.

The number one is in command.
The skipper's sick below,
A touch o' fever from the coast,
'As made the old man so;
But 'e's passed the word to the engineer,
"For Gawd's sake make 'er go!"

The "gen'ral quarters" sounded orf,
The bugler's made a call
(A call that means the "red" marines.
With fifty rounds of ball,
Are goin' to git a medal an' clasp.
Or an ensign for a pall!)

The number one is on the bridge.
The sun is low an' red!
An' shot an' shell, like fiends of 'ell,
Are shriekin' round 'is 'ead.
An' three marines are crippled.

An' their sergeant-major's dead!

The number one is on the bridge,
The dhow's a battered sight;
'Er rascal chief 'as come to grief;
'E's fought 'is final fight.
But the number one lies on the bridge.
An' 'is face is ghastly white.

A smile is on 'is bloodless lips,
'Is sword 'angs from 'is wrist.
And a lock of 'air of a maiden fair.
Is clasped in 'is bloodstained fist.
But 'e'll meet 'er at the great roll-call,
When they muster by "open list"!

BRITANNIA TO HER FIRST-BORN
I am no maiden, highly strung,
To faint, when bloody death is nigh.
I have not lived, by might of tongue
Nor by vain boastings, wind-wide flung!
But on fame's endless ladder, I
Have fought my way, from rung to rung!

I am no fretful, whimp'ring miss;
I am a woman, learned of years.
And once I felt your baby kiss:
Your bliss for me had greater bliss!
Your youthful sorrows had my tears.
O son o' mine, remember this!

Your foes were mine, in those dear days:
Your friends were kind, and kin to me.
We parted—so, we will not raise
The long dead years. We went our ways,
I, brooding by the cold grey sea;
You, pride-flushed, with your new-won bays!

The years have passed; it does but seem
As yester-eve you left my side.
I journeyed with you, dream on dream—
I heard your great war eagle's scream!
And on sweet Progress, your fair bride,
I saw the sun of Fortune's beam!

I mourned your follies, word and deed;
I watched your rising, when you rose.
By sober prayer, by Cross and Bead;
Until you found that greater Creed,

That in the broader channel flows.
The lowly truths, that higher lead!

You are my son, and born of me.
My laws of Right are Laws to you
Whose hands were stained in blood, to be
The hands that set the slave-man free!
And now, again, you dare and do—
For Justice, and Humanity!

The days to be are big with Fate!
Go fight your battle. Son o' mine:
And State to Shire, and Shire to State,
Its better self shall dedicate!
So, let the wily foe combine.
Whilst, hand-locked, heart-locked, we can wait!

TOMMY TO HIS LAUREATE
(Capetown, January 25, 1898)

O good-mornin', Mister Kiplin'! You are welcome to our shores:
To the land of millionaires and potted meat:
To the country of the "fonteins" (we 'ave got no "bads" or "pores"),
To the place where di'monds lay about the street
At your feet;
To the 'unting-ground of raiders indiscreet.

1 suppose you know this station, for you sort of keep in touch
With Tommy wheresoever 'e may go;
An' you know our "bat's" a shandy, made of 'Ottentot an' Dutch,
It's a language which is 'ideous an' low.
Don't you know
That it's "Wacht-een-beitje" 'stead of "'Arf a mo'?"

We should like to come an' meet you, but we can't without a pass;
Even then we'd 'ardly like to make a fuss;
For out 'ere, they've got a notion that a Tommy isn't class;
'E's a sort of brainless animal, or wuss!
Vicious cuss!
No, they don't expect intelligence from us.

You 'ave met us in the tropics, you 'ave met us in the snows;
But mostly in the Punjab an' the 'Ills.
You 'ave seen us in Mauritius, where the naughty cyclone blows.
You 'ave met us underneath a sun that kills.
An' we grills!
An' I ask you, do we fill the bloomin' bills?

Since the time when Tommy's uniform was musketoon an' wig.

There 'as always been a bloke wot 'ad a way
Of writin' of the Glory an' forgettin' the fatig',
'Oo saw 'im in 'is tunic day by day.
Smart an' gay,
An' forgot about the smallness of his pay!

But you're our partic'lar author, you're our patron an' our friend.
You're the poet of the cuss-word an' the swear.
You're the poet of the people, where the red-mapped lands extend,
You're the poet of the jungle an' the lair,
An' compare.
To the ever-speaking voice of everywhere!

There are poets wot can please you with their primrose-vi'let lays.
There are poets wot can drive a man to drink;
But it takes a "pukka" poet, in a Patriotic Craze,
To make a chortlin' nation squirm an' shrink.
Gasp an' blink;
An' 'eedless, thoughtless people stop an' think!

Yes, the 'and wot banged the banjo an made Tommy comic songs,
'Oo wrote of Empires, "Lion's 'Ead to Line,"
'Oo found an 'idden poem in M'Andrew's Injin gongs.
Was the checkin' 'and wot gave the warnin' sign.
In a line—
That gave the people soda after wine.

THE MISSION THAT FAILED
Our troop was encamped by the side of a stream
An' a very smart troop were we.
We 'ad Cavalry orficers—straight from town,
An' we escorted Mister Commissioner Brown,
Commissioner Brown, C.B.
An' we 'eard that the Governor put 'im down.
For a spare K.C.M.G.!

We wos camped near by to a border town.
On the borders of Creegerland—
A very despotic, republican state—
An' there we 'ad got the order to wait.
But why, we did not understand.
So we bedded our 'orses, an' cussed at our fate
(For you can't cuss the man in command).

One mornin' sez Mister Commissioner Brown,
Sez 'e to the 'ole parade,
"I've bin inspired by a dream just now—
I can't say why, an I can't say 'ow—
But a voice in my dream it said,

'O in Joannistown there's a deuce of a row
And badly they want your aid!'"

Now Joannistown is in Creegerland,
Which same is a friendly state.
An' it isn't no joke—which is puttin' it fine—
To pass without notice the border-post sign;
But we did it, as I will relate.—
We really intended to drop 'em a line!
But we 'adn't got time to wait.

We 'ad ridden some miles into Creegerland
When Commissioner Brown, C.B.,
'E called an 'alt,—which a troop requires.
For a man, 'e tires, as 'is 'orse perspires,—
An' 'e sez to the troop, sez 'e,
"About ten miles from 'ere are some telegraph wires,
An' a very good thought struck me.

"For fear of my dream bein' misunderstood
An' the evil constructions of liars!—
For fear of alarmin' the dear farmers' wives
An' disturbin' the quiet an' peace of their lives,
I think we will sever them wires!
An' I'll give somethin' 'andsome to 'im 'oo contrives
To cut off the current—with pliers!"

An' Michael M'Carty, Lance-Corp'ral was 'e.
Right guide to a section of "A,"
Started orf on the job, an' we whispered a cheer.
An' we each gave the beggar our flasks—full of beer—
To 'elp for to lighten 'is way!
We gave 'im cheap drinks—though it was very dear
When it came round to settling day!

M'Carty 'e rode, an' M'Carty 'e swilled.
An' M'Carty got big in the 'ead.
Till 'e couldn't tell telegraph poles from trees.
An' 'e wandered around, sorter go-as-you-please
Till 'is wonderin' wanderin's led
To the wires—of a fence! an' reclinin' at ease
'E cut up these wasters instead!

It's all over now: an' Brown 'e got jugged.
And the Burghers of Creegerland knowed.
They licked us to fits in a sweet little fight.
An' the King of Jerusalem wired 'is delight!
An' the Laureate wrote us an Ode!
An' Europe got ready for action that night
'Cos M'Carty got drunk on the road!

M'Carty's a thief, M'Carty's a beast,
An' M'Carty is likewise a liar!
'E went an' got drunk, which 'e shouldn't 'ave done;
'E went an' got drunk, an' 'e spoilt the 'ole fun:
An' the moral to them wot conspire
Is, Don't send a beer-swilling son of a gun
When you're cuttin a telegraph wire!

THE PRAYER

O God of Battles! Lord of Might!
A sentry, in the silent night,
I, 'oo 'ave never prayed.
Kneel on the dew-damp sands, to say,
O see me through the comin' day—
But, please remember, though I pray.
That I am not afraid!

O God of Battles! Lord of Might!
'Ere in the dusky, starry light.
My inner self I've weighed;
An' I 'ave seen my guilt an' sin;
I'm black as black can be, within.
But though I would forgiveness win.
It ain't 'cos I'm afraid!

O God of Battles! Lord of Might!
Keep me, to-morrow, in Your sight!—
Far 'ave I erred an strayed.
I've flaunted You, with gibe an' sneer,
At 'ome, with chums to laugh and cheer,
But now, I am alone—out 'ere!
But still I ain't afraid!

O God of Battles! Lord of Might!
The en'my's camp-fires twinkle bright.
To-morrow, Lord, Your aid;
The canteen was my Sunday-school:
The drill-book was my Golden Rule;
Wot are they now? O 'elpless fool!
But still, I'm not afraid!

O God of Battles! Lord of Might!
The price of every thoughtless slight
To-morrow will be paid!
A voice is whisp'rin to my 'eart—
A voice that makes me sweat an' start!-
"To-morrow, soul an' soldier part!"
But I—I'm not afraid!

O God of Battles! Lord of Might!
'Ere, in the silence of the night.
My 'umble prayer is prayed!
All life an' death are one to you!
If I must die—O 'elp me to!
In that last moment, see me through—
My God! I am afraid!

CEASE FIRE

The fight was done an hour ago:
The whole brigade has fallen back,
And I've been wand'rin' to and fro^
A-askin' any—white or black,
"Say—have you seen my brother. Jack?
His troop was first in the attack!"

I should have seen him here by now:
An hour ago the "cease fire" went.
He isn't wounded any'ow,
'Cos with the stretcher squads I went.
An' all my other time I've spent
A-hangin' round the doctor's tent.

Among the huddledj fallen men
I picked a way across the plain.
I got a dozen yards, an' then
Came back for fear I 'd turn my brain....
The mangled horrors of the slain!
O Christ! I can't go there again!

Say, have you seen my brother Jack?
Don't know! an' damn you, don't much care!-
But'scuse me, chum, a-talkin' back,
I'm sorter flustered with the glare.
These sands are hot, an' so's the air—
Perhaps he's doin' guard somewhere!

Old mother said before we went,
"Be sure you keep him in your sight.
(Not knowin' what a campaign meant).
"Don't let him stay out late o' night!"—
I wonder if he funked the fight
An' bolted. O pray God he might!

They're layin' out our dead just now,
He can't be, no, that—that ain't sense,
An' when he comes there'll be a row!
A-keepin' me in this suspense!
'Tis here our line of killed commence,

I'll sorter look—for make-pretence!

Pretendin' some one's here I know—
I'm half inclined to turn aback—
But one by one, along I go.
And see the crimson clottin' black....
His troop was first in the attack!
What! Jack! Is this—this Thing our Jack?

TOMMY'S AUTOGRAPH

I 'ad lorst my situation, an' the girl she got the 'ump.
An' the naggin' of my muvver nearly drove me orf my chump.
So I 'oofed it down to Woolwich, to the old recruitin' starf.
An' they give to me a paper for to fix my autygrarf!

Just to fix my autygrarf!
Lor' you should a 'eard me larf!
For the blessed Sergeant-Major wos a-tryin' on 'is chaff.
Didn't mind the Doctor's soundin's,
Nor 'is soap an' water barf!
But the fing as knocked me silly wos that bloomin' autygrarf!

I wos took before the colonel, an' I took a Bible oaf
That I 'd serve my Queen an' country, an' be square unto them boaf.
Then they got a printed paper, an' this Colonel on the starf
Sez, "You'll kindly read this over, an' affix your autygrarf!"

To affix my autygrarf!
Larf! You orter 'eard me larf!
Signin' fings like "Enry Irvin," Knight Commornder of the Barf!
Made me want to do a swagger
Like a Piccadilly calf!
On'y fancy! People wantin' Tommy Atkins' autygrarf!

Then I signs my name an' birfplace, an' the county I wos from,
An' I dots the "i" in Atkins, an' I crorst the "t" in tom.
A recruit is wurf a dollar, an' the sergeant gets an 'arf;
Just for 'andin' me a paper for to put my autygrarf!

Just to put my autygrarf!
Larf? You should 'ave 'eard them larf!
From the colonel wiv 'is spurs on, to the sergeant in 'is scarf.
When I sez, "Wot's this for, mister?"
Sez the colonel, "Go to Barf!"
"Don't you know the Queen is anxious for to get your autygrarf?"

I 'ave autygrarfed for clobber, I 'ave autygrarfed for pay;
I 'ave signed it wiv a flourish, I 'ave signed it wiv a "j"
On an Army Temperance pledge-book

(O the straight an' narrer parf!)—
To a "drunk" fine in the pay list, I've affixed my autygrarf!

Wot a name! An autygrarf!
'Nuff to drive a feller darf;
Callin' Christian name an "auty" an' the uvver name a "grarf,"
Writin' in a pocket-ledger—
'Stead of album bound in calf—
"Doo to soldier: Nil" (that's Latin), an' your bloomin' autygrarf!

AT THE BRINK!

'Tis now, as we tighten the girth,
'Tis now, as we buckle the sword.
When bitterness hardens our mirth,
'Tis now that we seek you, O Lord!
Give us hope now the future is black.
From fatuous arrogance ward—
The words that we cannot hold back!
Give peace in our time, O Lord!

You know of the hate—folly born;
You know of the wrath—money bred;
The impotent rage, and the scorn.
The trust and the faith that are dead.
Lest sorrow should spring from the land—
The crop of the seed of the sword—
O, stay the imperious hand;
Give peace in our time, O Lord!

'Tis good when the man loves the land,
'Tis good when he falls for his creed.
But woe to the hate that is fanned
By folly begotten of greed.
When the weak become foolishly strong.
When peoples, unwitting, applaud,—
The folly wrought wrong—still is wrong!
Give peace in our time, O Lord!

When the voice in the senate is stilled;
When the councillor speaks in a tent;
When the lands are untended, untilled;
What use if the stubborn relent?
What gain will the simpleton's shame,
The shrifts and lamentings, afford?
To-day, on their conduct, the blame;
Give peace in our time, O Lord!

Give peace: that is rooted in Right.
Give peace: that is strengthened by Grace.

Give peace: that we stand in your sight,
Thrice over a justified race.
'Tis peace—and with honour—we need.
And the child of our child shall award
The praise for our failing, or deed.
Give peace in our time, O Lord!

THE KING OF OOJEE-MOOJEE

We 'ave stowed our ammunition, we 'ave taken in our store,
An' our very last instructions we 'ave 'ad by semy-fore;
The Flagship's made a signal, "We wish you all success,"
An' we're off to Oojee-Moojee on the armoured cruiser "Bess."

For the King of Oojee-Moojee
Is a-comin of is tricks,
'E's cheeked the English Consul,
An 'e's chucked 'is wooden bricks.
'E won't do kindergarden.
An' 'e's done 'is lessons wrong;
Altogether Oojee-Moojee
Is a-comin of it strong!

An' the Point is miles be'ind us, an' 'eadquarters furder still;
We've exchanged a friendly greetin' wi' the bloke on Signal 'Ill;
We are off to Oojee-Moojee, an' we cannot be detained.
For relations dip-lo-matic 'ave become a trifle strained!

Now the King of Oojee-Moojee is a little coloured kid;
An' 'e rules some thousand niggers, an' 'e does as 'e is bid!
For the Government of England, with 'is interests in view,
'As civilised 'is country—an' collects 'is revenue!

For the King wot reigned afore 'im was an 'eathen nigger thief.
So we sent a missionary, for to teach 'im our belief.
(To prevent misunderstandin's, an' avoid unpleasant scenes.
We likewise sent an 'Otchkiss, an' a 'undred red marines.)

'E wouldn't take our gospel, an' unpleasantness arose.
Which cost six whites, and niggermen proportionate to those;
An' we left the King a-swingin' from a 'lyptus tree above.
Just to show as there was iron underneath the velvet glove.

Then our skipper very kindly did an 'andsome sort of thing.
For 'e made a proclamation that the nevvy of the King—
A funny little kiddy, with a sat-on sorter face—
Should rule the Oojee-Moojee, an' should take 'is uncle's place.

So we dressed 'im up in velvets, an' we fed 'im up on buns.
An' we gave 'is bit of buntin' a salute of twenty guns,

An' we gave to 'im a doctor for to cure 'is chills an' croups;
With a tutor, an' a gen'ral for to organise 'is troops.

So 'is tutor taught 'im manners, an' the way to part 'is 'air,
An' the gen'ral, in 'is spare time, taught 'im proper ways to sware;
The doctor, to complete 'im, was a-teaching him to mill-
When 'is 'ighness put the veto on the Education Bill.

Then 'e cheeked the British Consul!
Then 'e cussed the doctor's wife!
An' 'e chased 'is good, kind tutor, with a bloomin' carvin' knife;
Tore 'is books an' burnt 'is grammar (said they wasn't good for 'ealf).
Boned some whisky from the General, an' unchristianised 'isself!

So, we're hound for Oojee-Moojee,
An' we mus'n't he detained;
For relations dip-lo-matic
'Ave become a trifle strained:
"Situations complicated"—
"Warship ordered to the scene!"—
Just because a nigger kiddy's
Playin' truant with the Queen!

THE SONG OF THE TOWN

Sing hey! for the sand-freckled plain;
Sing ho! for the flower-flushed valley;
A song for the ship-sprinkled main.
And the sports where the wanderers rally,
A song for the lawn sloping down—
The lawn with its terrace and fountain.
But here's a song of the square white Town
By the mist-wrapped, cloud-capped mountain!

The whitewashed, square-cut town,
By the grey-green wind-swept sea;
The moving throng.
And the motor gong,
These sing the song for me!

Sing hey! for the Town and its folk.
The comers, the goers, the stayers;
The just arrived waster, dead-broke.
The homeward-bound mummers and players;
The white man suspiciously dark!
The trooper-man, newly recruited;
The hand-bagged and frock-coated clerk.
The pioneer corded and booted!

The motley-peopled town!

Its raw and cultured folk.
Live, work, and play
'Twixt Mount and Bay,
And bear one equal yoke.

Sing hey! for the Town, and its dress.
The garbs of the twenty-one nations:
The Kafir in blanket—and less.
The lady in Paris "creations";
The-man-about-town, rather loud,
The nigger in checks somewhat rasher;
Here, fez to the turban is bow'd.
There, top-hat comes off to the "smasher."

The particoloured town.
Where plush and broadcloth meet:
Where Islam's green
And Worth-wrought sheen
Rub textures in the street!

Sing hey! for the Town, as a town,
A song of its bricks and its plaster;
The slum that is mouldering down—
The mansion that's rising the faster.
Sing hey! for its one-storied past,
Be-flagged, and be-stoeped, and be-whitened;
Its five-storied future more vast.
Its breadth to be broadened and heightened.

The grim old, prim old town,
A brand-new vestment wears.
And arc-lights purr
Where blue-gums were.
And the blanket-Kafir stares!

BY SIMON'S BAY
In the mountain fold
By the green-blue bay,
Where the waves are flecked
By the evening gold
At the close of day;
And the berg is decked
With a film of grey,
And the mountain's frown
On the darkening town—
My mem'ries stray.

By the fringing beach.
By the restless wave.

Is the straggling town.
And its limits reach
From the highest place
By the mountain's crown
To the mountain's base—
Where the waters lave.

Hopeful Town
By the Cape of Hope;
By the sandy slope
Where the Hills look down;
By the wind-swept kloof—
On the barrack, grim:
On the whitened roof.
On the garden trim:
On the restless Bay
Where the sea-fowl whirls
And the spume-dust swirls
To the Zephyr's whim—
At the close of day.

Darkening Bay,
Where ever lay
Alert to slip
From leashes taut
A blood-flecked hound
In the pale lean ship;
And where the sound
Of echoing boom
From far away
Is a full-mouthed bay.
As the quarry's found.

Mournful bay
In green and grey
I've thought on you
This many a day.

THE SQUIRE
Sir John of the Isles,
'E stood on 'is lands.
An' looked round 'is large estates:
The lands of waste, an' the lands of corn;
The rose-clad lands, an' the lands of thorn;
An' 'is many gun guarded gates.
Sir John of the Isles,

'E sez to T.A.,
'E sez to T.A., sez 'e,

"Oh, you an' your chum, the sailor-man.
Must scour the country as far as you can
For you are gamekeepers to me."

Sir John of the Isles,
'E sez to the swells—
The Downing Street frock-coated crew—
"You are stewards of mine, on Colonial land.
An' my tenants, with seventeen guns an' a band.
Shall pay their respects unto you!"

Sez John of the Isles
To one of the swells,
"Near the lands where you're goin' to be
Is the dusty estate of a crotchety cuss,
'Oo from time to time causes a great deal of fuss.
For 'e thinks 'e's better nor me."

Sez John of the Isles,
"The tenants 'e rules
Are a very peculiar lot.
'Is bailifs are 'Ollanders, chock full of guile.
An' they run the estate in a Guy-Foxy style.
Which is Dynamite, Treason and Plot!"

Sez John of the Isles,
"Don't mind 'is remarks,
For the land which is 'is—it was mine;
But 'e took it to Law in a court rather grim,
An' a kopje-'id jury decided for 'im!
An' awarded the land as a fine."

Sir John of the Isles,
'E sez to the swell,
"You're a gentleman, breedin' an birth,
An' in case of a row, without losin' your 'ead.
You may take my gamekeepers, an' mark 'is land red!
On the survey-map of the Earth!"

THE SEA-NATION
We rose, a people of the sea,
Nursed by the wind, and rocked by wave.
Our hard, rock-founded history.
Was born from stories of our brave.
And northern ice-blasts steeled our frames
When war was but the best of games.

We saw a Roman Empire fall.
And fell; but falling, learned to rise.

We heard the voice of Progress call,
And in our folly we were wise:
When Briton, Saxon, Norman, Dane,
Bequeathed their progeny the main.

And conquered joined with conqueror;
And Norman fire, with Saxon zeal
Combined; we swept the world before
The twanging bow, and clanging steel.
Tyrants unmurm'ring bore our yoke,
And braggarts thought before they spoke.

Then Iron Might took Right to wife;
And lo! our liberty was bom!
We revelled in the newer life
When King was mated by a pawn.
Men lived between, of mighty worth;
From Montfort's death to Cromwell's birth.

We bore the arrogance of kings.
But bravèd death in fear of God.
We rose from great, to greater things.
The weak grew potent at our nod.
And nations watched the scales of Fate,
To see where England threw her weight!

We took our seed to other climes,
And from it sprang by divers seas.
An Oak—that grew among the Limes!
An Oak—among the Blue-gum trees!
The Cactus left the land because
The Acorn brought its ordered laws.

And like a giant, bearing stings
Of gnats, who joy to see him wince.
We stand—the envy of the kings
Despised by every petty prince!
Who know, that while enduring yet.
We bear—but we do not forget.

We lived, and live! The world shall see
An inextinguishable flame.
The nations fade; but we shall be!
When Gaul and Teuton are a name!
For us the seven seas in one:
For landlocked hordes—oblivion
NATURE FAILS

You can eas'ly understand
That the green of medder-land
Doesn't strike the bloke that 'as to push the roller;

An' Nature at the best.
When you put 'er to the test.
Undiluted, is a very poor consoler.

An' the blue of summer skies
'As no beauties for the eyes
Of defaulters on parade in marehin' order;
An' the rainiest of morns
Brings no feelin's—'cept to corns.
Of a feller pickin' oakum with a warder.

Wot's the beauty of the spot,
When you're bein' drilled with shot?
Wot is Nature when you're checked for bein' dirty?
An' eternity's a blank
To a feller on the crank,
When ev'ry blessed minute seems like thirty!

Bein' punished for your deeds.
On fatig' a-pickin' weeds.
Can a bloke admire the beauties of the clover?
Does the sunset on the 'ills
Give defaulters any thrills
Except to know the day is nearly over.

Bein' frog-marched to the clink,
Does a feller stop to think
On the grass before 'is eyes so swif'ly runnin',
'Ow that ev'ry single blade
Is most wonderfully made
Wiv a skill beyond all artificial cunnin'?

An' you cannot pant for wars
When you're scrubbin' barrack floors,
Or get inspired on bully-beef an' biscuit:
It requires a poet's soul
When a feller's cartin' coal
To think 'isself in danger, an' to risk it.

Does a feller care a D—
For the friskin' of a lamb,
When 'e 'as to watch the friskin' thro' a gratin'?
Does the lowin' of the 'erds.
Or the twitterin' of the birds.
Soothe a feller when for punishment 'e's waitin'?

ENVOI
In the deepest pits of 'Ell,
Where the worst defaulters dwell
(Charcoal devils used as fuel as you require 'em).
There's some lovely coloured rays,

Pyrotechnical displays:
But you can't expect the burnin to admire 'em!

THE COLONEL'S GARDEN

There are gardins, an' there's gardins.
Some are good, an' some are not.
There are gardins in a glass 'ouse
Where the air is alius 'ot.
But whether on a winder-ledge.
Or in a flower-pot,
I'll back our Colonel's gardin
For to lick the bilin' lot.

There are gardners, an' there's gardners.
Some are great, an' some are small.
Some could change a bloomin' brickfield
To a Covent Gard'n ball!
There are some 'oo couldn't 'ardly
Fix a creeper to a wall!
But I'll back our Colonel's gardner,
Jerry Jordan, 'gin 'em all!

O the flowers they are lovely!
An' the roses they are fair;
An' the daisies they are winkin'
Thro' a lash of maiden-'air!
An' the lilies, tall an' naked—
The' it's little that they care!
An' the garden—under Jerry—
Is a place beyond compare!

There are flowers bloomin' early.
There are flowers bloomin' late;
There is 'oneysuckle climbin'
On the porchway, by the gate.
There's some cress an' mustard growin'
On a commissairy plate!
O the garden it is lovely—
That's when Jerry's on the straight!

O the garden it's neglected^
An' the pinks 'ave ceased to pink,
An' the petals they are droppin'.
An' the blooms they bend and sink.
O the flowers they are fadin'
Now that Jerry's took to drink!
O the flowers they're neglected—
Jerry Jordan's in the clink!

For the flowers will not blossom.
An' they don't give out no smells.
The convul'vus it is weepin'
From its verigated bells.
An' the lily's in hysterics,
An' she faints away in spells:
O there's weepin', an' there's wailin'—
Jerry Jordan's doin' cells!

O the path is rolled an' gravelled.
An' the gardin's fresh as rain.
An' the weeds that strewed the borders
They no longer there remain.
An' the flowers they are smilin'.
For they're out of all their pain;
An' the bees they 'um for gladness—
Jerry Jordan's out again!

THE PEOPLE TO CECIL JOHN RHODES
July 18, 1899

By the bond that binds the scattered folk to home.
We have come.
By the love to dear old England which you bear—
And we share.
By the knowledge of the Empire you extend—
Britain's friend!—
We are gathered, many thousand people, to
Welcome you!

We are strangers drawn together by one tie.
They and I,
Merely men who, having never met before.
Meet no more!
But a common cause has bridged the social breach,
Each to each
Has one soft word of fellowship to say,
Here to-day.

If you search among our numbers you will find
Every kind:
Dutchman, Briton, "Africander," and Malay
In array;
Christian, Mussulman, and he of Abram's seed—
Every creed:
With the worshippers of Sakyanumi's mud—
Mighty Budh.

But if every heart was melted, and when done

Moulded one—
If a welcome in a polyglotic tongue
Could be sung—
If one voice could speak our sentiments to-day.
We would say,
Very simply: "We are glad that you are come—
Welcome home!"

We have followed you, and watched your noble stand
For your land.
And your triumphs and your greatly troubled hourSj
Have been ours:
And our sympathetic wishes for your cause.
Have been yours:
Since the day on which you left us to go forth,
"For my North!"

We have followed you through many foreign ways.
In these days.
By the Nilus, on the Desert, new surveyed,
You have strayed:
By the Pyramids and palms of Cairo town.
Parched and brown:
By the quiet shades of Oxford, prim and green.
You have been.

In the stately city hall, in spirit we
Came to see
The cheering thousands testify belief.
In their Chief.
In the regal courts of Potsdam, at your side
We were tied.
By the tighter bond than kinship ever drew—
We and you!

If our hearts in concord melted and were run
Into one!
If a welcome in a polyglotic tongue,
Could be sung:
If two words could voice our sentiments to-day.
We would say—
Very simply, being glad that you are come—
"Welcome home!"

WHEN LONDON CALLS!
There's a voice that calls to Mecca, there's a voice that calls to Rome.
(O the Holiest of Holies! O the Temple and the Shrine!)
There's a bleating from a pasture, and it calls a wand'rer home.
(O the friskings of the yearlings, and the lowing of the kine!)

There's a penetrating whisper that can rise above the gale
From the cot of thatch and plaster, from the oaken-gabled hall.
From the limpid lake of silver in the verdant velvet vale.
From the shamrock and the heather,
Hear the call!

There's a voice that calls the waster, when the doors of home are shut.
(O the voice of club and chamber, and the arc-light burning blue!)
There's a voice that calls the trooper in his daub and wattle hut.
(O the midnight cabs that rattle from the Strand to Waterloo!)
There's a voice for ever calling from the Square and from the Slum,
From the Hornsey Rise to Brixton, from St. Saviour's to St. Paul's.
'Tis the never-changing message of the everlasting "Come"
To the brick and to the mortar.
London calls!

You may still the voice of conscience, and suppress the blush of shame.
(O the deed that made you outlaw! O the folly and the sin!)
But never man ignored it when the call to London came.
(The call from belfry tower! O the clanging, banging din!)
'Tis the wooded green of Greenwich with the deer among the fern.
'Tis the bleak blank streets of Lambeth, where the drizzling fog-mist falls.
It's a weary aching whisper, and it murmurs, "O return"
To the Elegance, the Squalor.
London calls!

'Tis the swelling roar of Epsom, with the backers seven deep.
(O the rush around the Corner, and the finish on the Straight!)
'Tis the tinkling hum of Henley as it snuggles down to sleep.
(O the light-lined laughing river, with its fairy-fancied fête!)
'Tis the growl of Ratcliffe Highway, 'tis the lisp of Rotten Row;
'Tis the beauty that entrances, 'tis the horror that appals;
'Tis the firemen's horses tearing to the midnight sky aglow;
It's a vague and restless—something.
London calls!

It is early morning Fleet Street, when the throbbing presses fly.
(O the Father of the Chapel! O the ticking, talking tape!)
'Tis the universal High Street, where the world may see and buy.
(O the steamboat of Newcastle! O the feather of the Cape!)
'Tis the heart of all creation, where the veins of commerce meet;
'Tis the centre seat in gall'ry, 'tis the booked and numbered stalls;
'Tis the barrow in Whitechapel, 'tis the brougham in Regent Street;
'Tis the Commonplace—the Novel.
London calls!

'Tis the glitter and the jingle on the Foreign Office stairs.
(O the starred and gartered Levee! O the Rulers of the Land!)
'Tis the crowd about the stretcher and the burden that it bears.
(O the ward in darkened silence! O the swiftly running sand!)
'Tis the message of the letter, 'tis the message of the wire;

'Tis the dainty hand that types it, 'tis the awkward fist that scrawls;
'Tis the memory that sickens, 'tis the thought that burns like fire;
'Tis the life that's worth the living!
London calls!

'Tis the cheering of the Commons and the cry of "Who goes home?"
(O the bell that rings Division! O the seat beneath the card!)
'Tis the choir-boys' voices rising to the lofty, painted dome.
(O the flutter of the pigeons in the flagged and mossy yard!)
'Tis the Sabbath bells that echo down the silent city streets;
'Tis the Steel inside the Velvet! 'Tis the stroking hand that mauls!
'Tis the Tutor, it's the Master. It prepares and it completes!
It is London—and its London!
And it calls!

CAIROWARDS

Going up—and by all one man's will!
Untrodden lands shall echo with our roars,
Our engines' wheels shall break the mountains' still.
Uncharted rivers see us by their shores;
And where the lions drink, and panthers prey.
Shall lie the ballast of our iron-bound way.

Going up! Primaeval forest, where
The Bushman lurks with poison at his lips.
Must give its best, and all its treasures bare.
When our iron-monster in its hollows dips;
And caves, from which the cobra issues forth,
Shall be a Somewhere Junction—for the North.

Going up! Eternal snows, that crown
The lonely summits of the lordly hills.
Shall look upon our laboured paths, and frown
Upon the girdered bridge that spans their rills;
But, clinging to the slope, with scanty hold.
The road shall be unfastened, fold by fold.

Going up! The stifling winds that blow
Across the sweep of fiery desert waste
Shall clog and cloy our workings as we go.
And strive to check us in our desp'rate haste.
With sand that holds us in its shifting clutch—
And iron and brass shall blister to the touch.

Going up! The Nile in sullen wrath
Shall rise and smite the sleeper from the rail.
And say: "Behold the Mistress of the North!
Who does not let the work of man prevail!"
But patient man shall strive against her might

Until the palms of Cairo are in sight!

Father of all!
Robèd in splendour,
Thou who dost wield
Almighty power.
All things are thine.
Fruitage and flower—
Cattle and kine—
Vineyard and field!
Hear, when we call.
Praising the Sender!

Father of all!
Strong to deliver!
Here, do we place,
Down at Thy feet,
Fruits of our hands—
Trophies of wheat,
Won from Thy lands—
Trophies of chase.
Hear, when we call.
Praising the Giver!

Father of all!
Weaver and fuller;
Craftsman and herd;
Chapman and knave;
Worker and drone;
Headman and slave.
Worship a-prone—
Bow to Thy word!
Hear Thou our call.
Praising the Ruler!

Father of all!
Billow and breaker
Sink to Thy nod!
Here, have we brought.
That which we found,
That which we wrought,
Drawn from Thy ground.
Culled from Thy sod.
Hear, when we call.
Praising the Maker!

Father of all!
Thine is the story

Written in space!
What Thou hast made
Knows not of death.
Let us not fade.
Catching Thy breath.
Live by Thy grace!
Hear Thou our call.
Thine is the Glory!

Edgar Wallace – A Short Biography

Richard Horatio Edgar Wallace was born on the 1st April 1875 at 7 Ashburnham Grove, Greenwich. His mother, Mary Jane "Polly" Richards was born into an Irish Catholic family in Liverpool in 1843 and had worked in theatres, both as an actress in bit-parts and as a stagehand and usherette, until she married a Merchant Navy Captain, Joseph Richards, in 1867. He too had been born into an Irish Catholic family in Liverpool. His father had also been a Captain in the Merchant Navy, and his mother's family had a marine background. Mary was eight months pregnant with Joseph's child when he died at sea, and it was once the child had been born that she first turned to the stage, taking the stage name Polly Richards.

She joined the Marriott family theatre troupe in 1872. It was managed by Mrs. Alice Edgar, Richard Edgar, Grace Edgar, Adeline Edgar and Richard Horatio Edgar, Wallace's father. In late 1874 Mary and Richard Horatio Edgar had a brief sexual encounter at the party following a successful show, and she fell pregnant. Worried about the scandal which would ensue and fearing that she might forever lose her job at the troupe, she fabricated an obligation in Greenwich would detain her there for at least six months. She lived in a room in the boarding house on Ashburnham Grove until her son, Edgar, was born. She had already made preparations through her midwife for a couple to foster the child, and when Edgar was born the midwife presented her with Mrs Freeman. Her husband was a fishmonger at Billingsgate market and she already had ten children. She was happy to foster the child and for Polly to make frequent visits to see him in exchange for a small sum of money which Polly made from her work in the theatre troupe.

Wallace was now known as Richard Horatio Edgar Freeman, taking his father's forenames and his foster family's surname. Broadly speaking his childhood was a happy one. The Freemans looked after him lovingly and he had good friendships with his foster siblings, particularly Clara Freeman, twenty years his senior, who often looked after him as a child. After a few years Polly's finances tightened and she was no longer in a position to afford the fee she had been paying the Freemans. However, they had grown to love the young Wallace and opted to adopt him in order to keep him out of the workhouse. Polly could no longer visit him. George Freeman was keen to ensure that he had equal opportunities and did all he could to secure him an education at St. Alfege with St. Peter's, a Peckham boarding school. Despite his adoptive father's efforts, though, Wallace left the school aged twelve for truancy.

Instead he went to work and by the time he was fourteen or fifteen he had experience selling newspapers at Ludgate Circus, near Fleet Street, as a worker in a rubber factory, as a shoe shop assistant, as a milk delivery boy and as a ship's cook. He stole from the milk company which resulted in his dismissal, and in 1894 was engaged to a local girl from Deptford named Edith Anstree, though he broke this off and instead joined the Infantry. He adopted the name Edgar Wallace which he took from Lew Wallace, the author of *Ben-Hur*, and his medical record records a diminutive 33" chest and a stunted growth. his first posting was with the West Kent Regiment in South Africa in 1896, though he did not enjoy military life, arranging to be transferred to the Royal Army Medical Corps. Though this was a less strenuous job, it was also significantly less pleasant and so he again transferred to the Press Corps, which he found suited him far better.

He was in Cape Town in 1898 where he met Rudyard Kipling and was inspired to begin writing and publishing poetry and songs. His first collection of ballads, *The Mission that Failed!* and was enough of a success that in 1899 he paid his way out of the armed forces in order to turn to writing full time. His first work was as a war correspondent for Reuters who kept him in Africa to cover the Boer War, and then for the Daily Mail in 1900 and various other periodicals after that. It was while he was in South Africa that he met and married Ivy Maude Caldecott, who was 21 when they married in 1901, despite her Wesleyan missionary father's strong opposition to the union, for several reasons, one of which was that Wallace's writing was not turning quite the profit he had expected it would. *War and Other Poems* and *Writ in Barracks,* both published in 1900, had not proved as popular as his first collection. Eleanor Clare Hellier Wallace, their first child, died of meningitis in 1903 and, in rather deep debt, they returned to London. Wallace used his contacts with the Daily Mail to get work with them in London, electing to write detective novels as a means of making quick money.

Wallace met Polly, his birth mother, in 1903. He didn't remember her from his childhood as he had been too young when she became unable to visit, so it was as though they were meeting for the first time. She was sixty years old and terminally ill, living in abject poverty. She had come to Wallace seeking financial support, but he turned her away. She died in the Bradford Infirmary later that year. In 1904 he and Ivy had a son, Bryan. He was still writing and had completed his first thriller, *The Four Just Men*. Since nobody would publish it he resorted to setting up his own publishing company which he called Tallis Press and he published a serialised version of *The Four Just Men* in 1905. He received promotional assistance from the Daily Mail in which he ran a competition for entrants to guess the method of murder in the final chapter, with a prize of £1,000 for a correct guess. Although the paper's proprietor, Lord Alfred Harmsworth, refused Wallace the £1,000 prize money, Wallace persisted and went ahead with the competition, recklessly advertising on billboards and buses all over the country, hoping to expand his advertisements across the Empire. His worried colleagues at the Daily Mail managed to convince him to lower the prize money to £500, split into a first prize of £250, a second prize of £200 and a third of £50, but with the total cost of his advertisements nearing £2,000 he would need to sell £2,500 worth of copies before he could see any profit. He was confident that this could be achieved in just three months.

Though he had remarkable enthusiasm, it became clear that his managerial skills left a lot to be desired. It soon emerged that nowhere in the competition terms and conditions had he included a clause limiting the competition to one single winner; instead, any entrant with a winning answer was entitled to their corresponding prize money. Thus, if ten entrants guessed the first prize answer, the competition was obliged to pay each entrant £250. This error was only noticed after the competition had been closed and the solution had been printed in the final installment of the novel, meaning that not only was there no opportunity to write his way out of enormous financial obligation, but the entrants who had guessed correctly would by now have read the final chapter and know they had done so. £250 was an enormous amount of money to the average Edwardian family and those entitled to it were likely to make a lot of noise if they didn't receive their money. Despite this, Wallace's fist instinct was to attempt to ignore the issue entirely, even as he discovered that he initial calculations had been dramatically over-enthusiastic and it would take nearer to two years of continuous sales to break even at the initial cost of £2,500, let alone the new figure which included every correct guesser. Compounding the problem even further was the awful realisation that as sales continued throughout the initial three month period and Wallace approached the £2,500 break-even figure, new readers were still eligible to enter and guess correctly. Though it is unknown how much he eventually owed his readers, Lord Harmsworth found himself having to loan over £5,000 in order to protect the reputation of the newspaper, since 1906 had come around and there still hadn't been a list printed of all prize-winners. It was less a charitable act than one of a man anxious that the failure would reflect ill on his own paper. Wallace filed for bankruptcy shortly thereafter and as a token gesture to his creditors sold the rights to the novel to Sir George Newnes, a publisher and editor, for £75. In the midst of this chaos though, Wallace managed to write and published *Smithy*, which would become the first of a series of *Smithy* novels.

Following this fiascos Wallace was dismissed from the Daily Mail in 1907 when inaccuracies which were found in his reporting, resulting in libel cases being brought against the paper. That year he became the first reporter to be fired from the Daily Mail and was his awful reputation prevented him from finding work at any other papers. Despite all this, though, he travelled to the Congo Free State later that year and reported on the criminal treatment of the Congolese people by King Leopold II of Belgium and the Belgian rubber companies. Up to fifteen million Congolese were killed in various atrocities, and Wallace was asked to serialise stories based on his experiences for her penny magazine *Weekly Tale-Teller*. He and Ivy had another daughter, named Patricia, in 1908. Though his new work for *Weekly Tale-Teller* was bringing in some money, their financial situation was still dire and Ivy was occasionally forced to sell off her jewellery and possessions in order to pay for food. In 1911 his Congolese stories were published in a collection called *Sanders of the River*, which quickly became a bestseller. He would publish eleven more such collections featuring a total of 102 stories of adventure and tribal life set on the river Congo.

From 1908 he started to enjoy a revival of both his success and his reputation. The majority of his initial writing he sold outright in order to make money as quickly as possible and placate his creditors in the United Kingdom and South Africa, but as his success saw the reestablishment of his reputation he began to find work once again as a journalist, beginning in horse racing for the *Week-End*, the *Evening News* and then as an editor for the *Week-End Racing Supplement*. Following this success he started his own racing papers, *Bibury's* and *R. E. Walton's Weekly*, eventually buying his own racehorses and losing thousands gambling. His success was insufficient to support his newly extravagant lifestyle and his marriage began to fail in the light of his financial irresponsibility. He and Ivy had their last child together, Michael Blair Wallace, in 1916, and she filed for divorce in 1918 moving to Tunbridge Wells with her children.

Wallace began to fall for his secretary Ethel Violet King and they married in 1921, having a child, Penelope Wallace, in 1923, who would herself go on to become a successful crime writer. Wallace now began to take his career as a fiction writer more seriously, signing with Hodder and Stoughton in 1921. He now began to organize his contracts more carefully, arranging for royalties and properly organized promotions, run by people more business-minded than himself. He was marketed as the 'King of Thrillers' and they gave him the trademark image of a trilby, a cigarette holder and a yellow Rolls Royce. He was truly prolific, capable not only of producing a 70,000 word novel in three days but of doing three novels in a row in such a manner. His publishers signed off on almost everything he wrote as soon as he turned it in, estimating that by 1928 one in four books being read at any time was written by Wallace, for alongside his famous thrillers he wrote variously in other genres, including but not limited to science fiction, non-fiction accounts of WWI which amounted to ten volumes and screen plays. Eventually he would reach the remarkable total of 170 novels, 18 stage plays and 957 short stories.

Wallace became chairman of the Press Club which to this day holds an annual Edgar Wallace Award, rewarding 'excellence in writing'. In 1923 he broadcasted a report on the Epsom Derby horse race for the British Broadcasting Company, making him the first ever radio sports correspondent. His ex-wife Ivy had suffered from breast cancer between 1923-1924, and it eventually killed her in 1926 despite a successful operation to remove a tumour the year before. He wrote the essay "The Canker in our Midst" in 1926 which dealt, aggressively and controversially, with the problem of paedophilia in show business, describing how children were unwittingly left open to sexual abuse, and linking paedophilia with homosexuality. Its tone has been described as "intolerant, blustering, kick-the-blighters-down-the-stairs". He was appointed chairman of the British Lion Film Corporation on the back of the success of *The Ringer* and on the agreement that he give British Lion first choice on all his future work. This contract gave him an annual salary and a large amount of stock with the company, along with a stipend on all British Lion production of his work and 10% of their annual profits. This extraordinary contract gave him annual earnings by 1929 of almost £50,000, or almost £2 million in 2014.

He now became an active figure in politics, entering the 1931 general election as a Liberal contestant in Blackpool, rejecting the current government in favour of free trade. He lost the election by over 33,000 votes and went to America in late 1931, once again deeply in debt after buying the *Sunday News* which closed six months later. In America he quickly found work as a script doctor for RKO Pictures, enjoying early success with the 1932 adaptation of *The Hound of the Baskervilles*. This success, along with that of the play *The Green Pack*, established his reputation in America and he was able to see his own work adapted for film, beginning with *The Four Just Men*. His most successful theatrical work, *On The Spot*, which explores the life of Al Capone, has been described as "arguably, in construction, dialogue, action, plot and resolution, still one of the finest and purest of 20th-century melodramas". These successes led to his assignation on RKO's "gorilla picture" which would become famous as King Kong in 1933.

He worked on the first draft though he was beginning to experience severe headaches which brought about a diagnosis of diabetes. Despite taking medication to address his condition, it deteriorated in a matter of days. His wife booked him passage home but soon heard that he had entered a coma and died of his condition and double pneumonia on the 7th of February 1932 in North Maple Drive, Beverly Hills. In his honour the bell at St. Bride's church on Fleet Street tolled for the duration of the morning while the flags flew at half-mast. He was buried near his home in England at Chalklands, Bourne End, in Buckinghamshire. Once again, at the time of his death he was in severe debt, mostly to racing bookkeepers, though these debts were settled within two years thanks to the enormous royalties his estate continued to receive from his contracts. His writing has been translated into 29 languages, and is considered one of the most important bodies of Colonial writing.

Edgar Wallace – A Concise Bibliography

African Novels
Sanders of the River (1911)
The People of the River (1911)
The River of Stars (1913)
Bosambo of the River (1914)
Bones (1915)
The Keepers of the King's Peace (1917)
Lieutenant Bones (1918)
Bones in London (1921)
Sandi the Kingmaker (1922)
Bones of the River (1923)
Sanders (1926)

Again Sanders (1928)

Four Just Men (Series)
The Four Just Men (1905)
The Council of Justice (1908)
The Just Men of Cordova (1917)
The Law of the Four Just Men (US title: Again the Three Just Men) (1921)
The Three Just Men (1926)
Again the Three Just Men (US title: The Law of the Three Just Men) (1929) a.k.a. Again the Three

Mr. J. G. Reeder (Series)
Room 13 (1924)
The Mind of Mr. J. G. Reeder (US title: The Murder Book of Mr. J. G. Reeder) (1925)
Terror Keep (1927)
Red Aces (1929)[27]
The Guv'nor and Other Short Stories (US title: Mr. Reeder Returns) (1932)

Detective Sgt. (Inspector) Elk series
The Nine Bears or The Other Man or The Cheaters (1910)
revised as Silinski - Master Criminal (1930)
The Fellowship of the Frog (1925)
The Joker or The Colossus (1926)
The Twister (1928)
The India-Rubber Men (1929)
White Face (1930)

Educated Evans (Series)
Educated Evans (1924)
More Educated Evans (1926)
Good Evans (1927)

Smithy (Series)
Smithy (1905)
Smithy Abroad (1909)
Smithy and The Hun (1915)
Nobby or Smithy's Friend Nobby (1916)

Crime Novels
Angel Esquire (1908)
The Fourth Plague or Red Hand (1913)
Grey Timothy or Pallard the Punter (1913)
The Man Who Bought London (1915)
The Melody of Death (1915)
A Debt Discharged (1916)
The Tomb of T'Sin (1916)
The Secret House (1917)
The Clue of the Twisted Candle (1918)
Down under Donovan (1918)
The Man Who Knew (1918)
The Strange Lapses of Larry Loman (1918)
The Green Rust (1919)

Kate Plus Ten (1919)
The Daffodil Mystery or The Daffodil Murder (1920)
Jack O'Judgment (1920)
The Angel of Terror or The Destroying Angel (1922)
The Crimson Circle (1922)
Mr. Justice Maxwell or Take-A-Chance Anderson(1922)
The Valley of Ghosts (1922)
Captains of Souls (1923)
The Clue of the New Pin (1923)
The Green Archer (1923)
The Missing Million (1923)
The Dark Eyes of London or The Croakers (1924)
Double Dan or Diana of Kara-Kara (US Title) (1924)
The Face in the Night or The Diamond Men or The Ragged Princess (1924)
The Sinister Man (1924)
The Three Oak Mystery (1924)
The Blue Hand or Beyond Recall (1925)
The Daughters of the Night (1925)
The Gaunt Stranger or Police Work (1925) revised as The Ringer (1926)
A King by Night (1925)
The Strange Countess (1925)
The Avenger or The Hairy Arm (1926)
'The Black Abbot (1926)
The Day of Uniting (1926)
The Door with Seven Locks (1926)
The Man from Morocco or Souls In Shadows or The Black (US Title) (1926)
The Million Dollar Story (1926)
The Northing Tramp or The Tramp (1926)
Penelope of the Polyantha (1926)
The Square Emerald or The Woman (1926)
The Terrible People or The Gallows' Hand (1926)
We Shall See! or The Gaol-Breakers (US Title) (1926)
The Yellow Snake or The Black Tenth (1926)
Big Foot (1927)
The Feathered Serpent or Inspector Wade or Inspector Wade and the Feathered Serpent (1927)
Flat 2 (1927)
The Forger or The Counterfeiter (1927)
Terror Keep (1927)
The Hand of Power or The Proud Sons of Ragusa (1927)
The Man Who Was Nobody (1927)
Number Six (1927)
The Squeaker or The Sign of the Leopard or The Squealer (US Title) (1927)
The Traitor's Gate (1927)
The Double (1928)
The Flying Squad (1928)
The Gunner or Gunman's Bluff (US Title) (1928)
Four Square Jane or The Fourth Square (1929)
The Golden Hades or Stamped In Gold or The Sinister Yellow Sign (1929)
The Green Ribbon (1929)
The Calendar (1930)
The Clue of the Silver Key or The Silver Key (1930)

The Lady of Ascot (1930)
The Devil Man or Sinister Street or Silver Steel
or The Life and Death of Charles Peace (1931)
The Man at the Carlton or The Mystery of Mary Grier (1931)
The Coat of Arms or The Arranways Mystery (1931)
On the Spot: Violence and Murder in Chicago (1931)
When the Gangs Came to London or Scotland Yard's Yankee Dick
or The Gangsters Come To London (1932)
The Frightened Lady or The Case of the Frightened Lady or Criminal At Large (1933)
The Green Pack (1933)
The Man Who Changed His Name (1935)
The Mouthpiece (1935)
Smoky Cell (1935)
The Table (1936)
Sanctuary Island (1936)

Other Novels
Captain Tatham of Tatham Island or Eve's Island or The Island of Galloping Gold (1909)
The Duke in the Suburbs (1909)
Private Selby (1912)
"1925" - The Story of a Fatal Peace (1915)
Those Folk of Bulboro (1918)
The Book of all Power (1921)
Flying Fifty-five (1922)
The Books of Bart (1923)
Barbara on Her Own (1926)

Poetry Collections
The Mission That Failed (1898)
War and Other Poems (1900)
Writ In Barracks (1900)

Non-Fiction
Unofficial Despatches of the Anglo-Boer War (1901)
Famous Scottish Regiments (1914)
Field Marshal Sir John French (1914)
Heroes All: Gallant Deeds of the War (1914)
The Standard History of the War – Volumes 1 – 4 (1914)
Kitchener's Army and the Territorial Forces:
The Full Story of a Great Achievement (1915)
Vol. 2-4. War of the Nations (1915)
Vol. 5-7. War of the Nations (1916)
Vol. 8-9. War of the Nations (1917)
Famous Men and Battles of the British Empire (1917)
Tam of the Scouts (1918)
The Real Shell-Man: The Story of Chetwynd of Chilwell (1919)
People or Edgar Wallace by Himself(1926)
The Trial of Patrick Herbert Mahon (1928)
My Hollywood Diary (1932)

Screenplays

King Kong (1932, first draft of original screenplay, 110 pages) While the script was not used in its entirety, much of it was retained for the final screenplay.
The Hound of the Baskervilles (1932, British film)
The Squeaker (1930, British film)
Prince Gabby (1929, British film)
Mark of the Frog (1928, American film)
The Valley of Ghosts (192

Short Story Collections
The Admirable Carfew (1914)
The Adventure of Heine (1917)
Tam O' the Scouts (1918)
The Fighting Scouts (1919)
Chick (1923)
The Black Avons (1925)
The Brigand (1927)
The Mixer (1927)
This England (1927)
The Orator (1928)
The Thief in the Night (1928)
Elegant Edward (1928)
The Lone House Mystery and Other Stories (Collins and son, 1929)
The Governor of Chi-Foo (1929)
Again the Ringer The Ringer Returns (US Title) (1929)
The Big Four or Crooks of Society (1929)
The Black or Blackmailers I Have Foiled (1929)
The Cat-Burglar (1929)
Circumstantial Evidence (1929)
Fighting Snub Reilly (1929)
For Information Received (1929)
Forty-Eight Short Stories (1929)
Planetoid 127 and The Sweizer Pump (1929)
The Ghost of Down Hill & The Queen of Sheba's Belt (1929)
The Iron Grip (1929)
The Lady of Little Hell (1929)
The Little Green Man (1929)
The Prison-Breakers (1929)
The Reporter (1929)
Killer Kay (1930)
Mrs William Jones and Bill (1930)
Forty Eight Short-Stories (George Newnes Limited ca. 1930)
The Stretelli Case and Other Mystery Stories (1930)
The Terror (1930)
The Lady Called Nita (1930)
Sergeant Sir Peter or Sergeant Dunn, C.I.D. (1932)
The Scotland Yard Book of Edgar Wallace (1932)
The Steward (1932)
Nig-Nog and other humorous stories (1934)
The Last Adventure (1934)
The Woman From the East (1934) Co-written By Robert George Curtis
The Edgar Wallace Reader of Mystery and Adventure (1943)

The Undisclosed Client (1963)

Other
King Kong, with Draycott M. Dell, (1933), 28 October 1933 Cinema Weekly

Plays
An African Millionaire (1904)
The Forest of Happy Dreams (1910)
Dolly Cutting Herself (1911)
The Manager's Dream (1914)
M'Lady (1921)
Double Dan (1926)
The Mystery of room 45 (1926)
A Perfect Gentleman (1927)
The Terror (1927)
Traitors Gate (1927)
The Lad (1928)
The Man Who Changed His Name (1928)
The Squeaker (1928)[27]
The Calendar (1929)
Persons Unknown (1929)
The Ringer (1929)
The Mouthpiece (1930)
On the Spot (1930)
Smoky Cell (1930)
The Squeaker (1930)
To Oblige A Lady (1930)
The Case of the Frightened Lady (1931)
The Old Man (1931)
The Green Pack (1932)
The Table (1932)

www.ingramcontent.com/pod-product-compliance
Lightning Source LLC
Chambersburg PA
CBHW061502170626
46811CB00004B/1591

* 9 7 8 1 7 8 3 9 4 4 8 9 7 *